To...

with a heart
full of love

Love is all around St. Louis

Published by Sourcebooks Jabberwocky, an imprint of Sourcebooks, Inc.
P.O. Box 4410, Naperville, Illinois 60567-4410
(630) 961-3900
Fax: (630) 961-2168
www.sourcebooks.com

Source of Production: Phoenix Color, Hagerstown, Maryland
Date of Production: August 2015
Run Number: 5004410
Printed and bound in the United States of America.
PHC 10 9 8 7 6 5 4 3 2 1

Love is all around St. Louis

Written by Wendi Silvano

Illustrated by Joanna Czernichowska

sourcebooks
jabberwocky

Love is a feeling that comes from inside.

Everyone feels it. It can't be denied.

But how do we know that it's there? What's the clue?

How can we see it?

Just what can we do?

Love's all around, if you just pay attention,

in people and places too many to mention.

Go look at the **park,**

on the **street,**

at the **mall.**

You'll see love all over. It's **big** and it's small!

All through **St. Louis,** in cars and on trains,

in taxis and buses, on boats and on planes,

in **Kirkwood,** and **Soulard,**
and **Southampton** too,

you'll find there is **love** that will come into view.

Missouri
River

Right there, on the lawn, in cool Suson Park

is a **mom** with her **babe**,

hearing songs of a lark.

She **swaddles** him, **cuddles** him, **kisses** his ear.

That surely is **love**, it's perfectly clear!

At a store in Creve Coeur, a girl gets a bear.

She squeezes him,

squishes him,

ruffles his hair.

It's clear that she **loves** him. She's **smiling** and bright.
She tucks him in **softly** and **gently** at night.

That same little girl, the very next day,

sees a **friend** at her school who is too **sad** to play.

So she sits down beside him and **listens** and **shares**,

making sure that he knows there's someone who **cares**.

Now the boy who was **sad** feels much **better**, you see,

so he runs home all happy to play with **Magee**.

They **romp** and they **frolic**.

They **fetch** and they **run**.

It's certain he **loves** him. They're having such **fun!**

You can see how **love** travels
when **shared** with a friend.
If *everyone* shares love, it never will end.
From one to another, it s p r e a d s and it grows.
You can't have *too much*, as everyone knows.

An officer in Midtown who **helps** change a flat.

A fireman in Clayton who **rescues** a cat.

BUSCH STADIUM

The home team that makes the crowd **cheer** and **clap.**

Each moment has **love** like a **gift** you unwrap.

There's a **father** who sits at the table each night,
helping out with the homework to get it just **right**.
He's tired and busy, but that's **love,** you know...
giving up what you want to **help** someone else **grow**.

It's not only *people* who show love, it's true.

Just come take a look in

the St. Louis Zoo.

The polar bear tumbles

and rolls with her cub,

and when they are finished,

she gives him a rub.

Where else is there **love?** Have we looked all around?

I think we've forgotten—love grows from the ground!

In the **meadows** and **gardens** and parks you will find

that the earth shows us **love** of all shapes and all kinds.

Wherever you look, love comes into sight.

It's there in the morning, it's there in the night.

But in all of St. Louis,

the best love you'll find

is a love that is gentle,

and selfless, and kind...

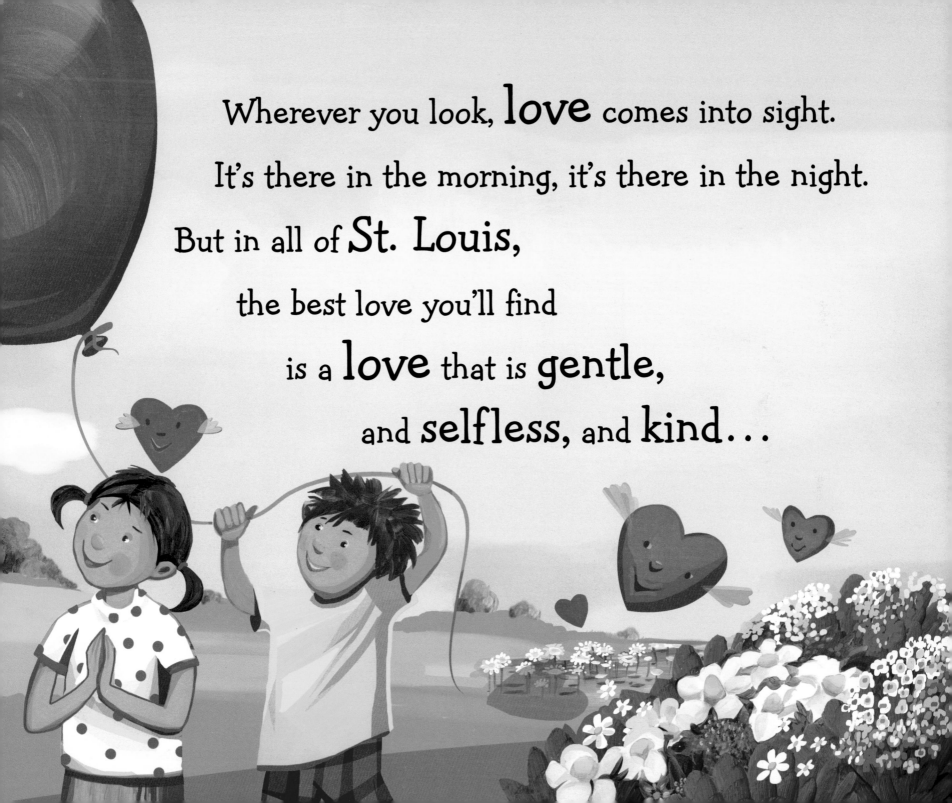

It's the love found at home. It shows up each day
in things people do and in things people say.
There's no greater love, I can tell you, it's true,
than the love of your family...

Especially for YOU!